This book belongs to

Disney

Written by Bonnie Brooke

Laughing All the Way

Laugh and cheer —

winter's here!

zippers, snaps,

and boots, and caps!

Gracefully glide

and slip and slide!

Games on ice with friends are nice.

Dashing through snow!

Here we go!

Hold on tight!

What a sight!

Roll and climb.

Snowball time!

Laugh and play
all the way!

...and all for fun!

Merry Christmas, everyone!